From My Window

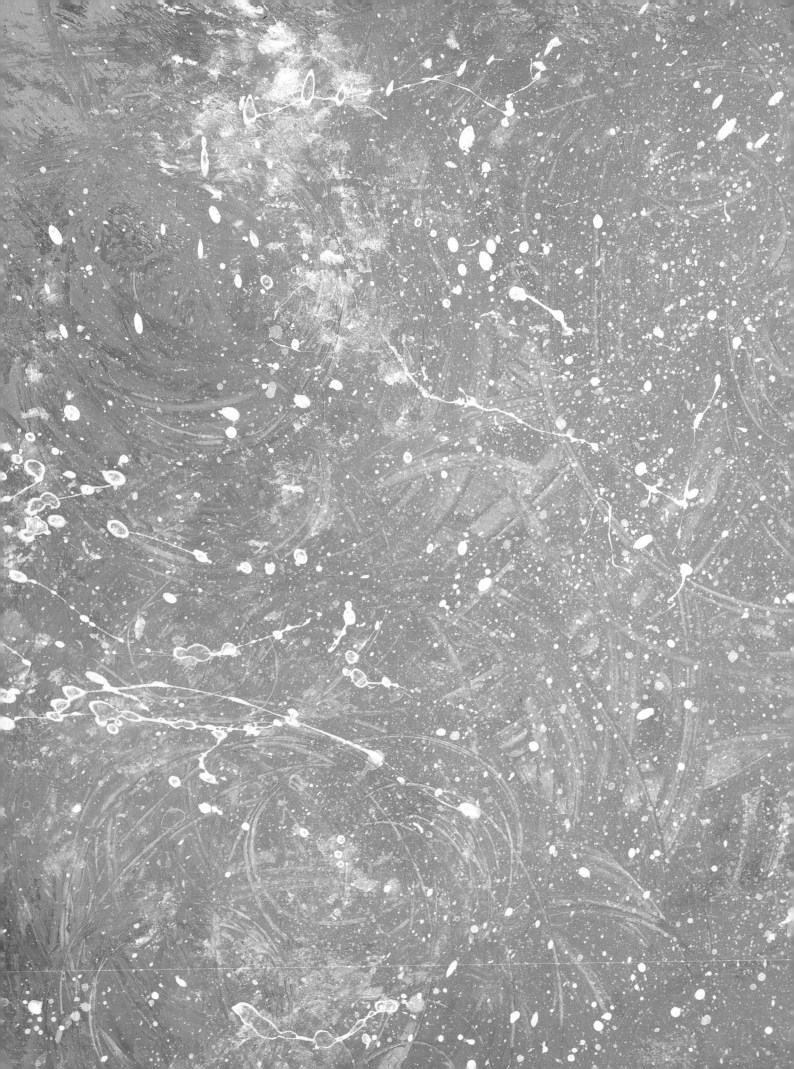

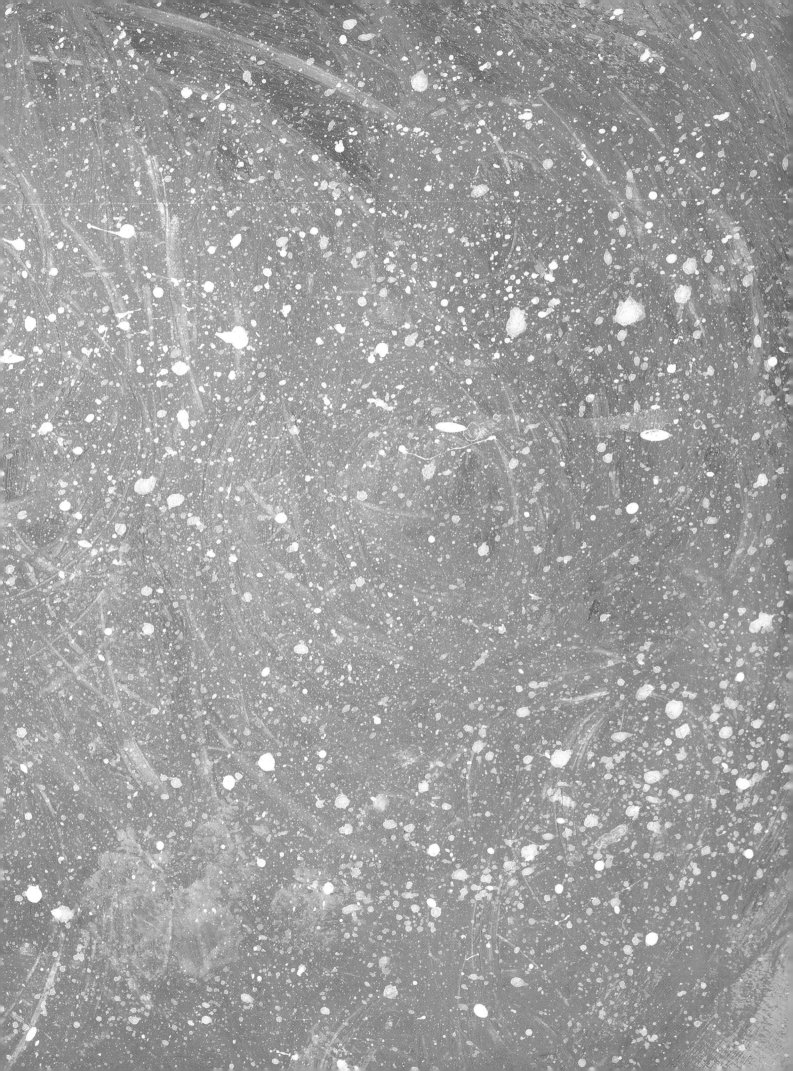

© 1995 Silver Burdett Press
Illustrations © 1995 Anna Rich

© Copyright, 1985, 1974, Ginn and Company
Theodore Clymer, Adviser

Published by Silver Press,
an imprint of Silver Burdett Press,
A Simon & Schuster Company
299 Jefferson Road
Parsippany, NJ 07054

Printed in the United States of America

10 9 8 7 6 5 4 3 2 1

Library of Congress Cataloging-in-Publication Data
Wong, Olive
    From My Window/by Olive Wong; illustrated by
Anna Rich.
        p. cm.
    Summary: A boy looks out at snow, trees, people,
and other things from his apartment window.
    (1. City and town life—Fiction.) I. Rich, Anna.
1956- ill. II. Title.
PZ7.W8423Fr   1995
(E)—dc20   94-20303   CIP   AC
ISBN 0-382-24665-9 (LSB) ISBN 0-382-24666-7 (JHC)
ISBN 0-382-24667-5 (S/C)

From My Window

by Olive Wong

illustrated by Anna Rich

Silver Press

Parsippany, New Jersey

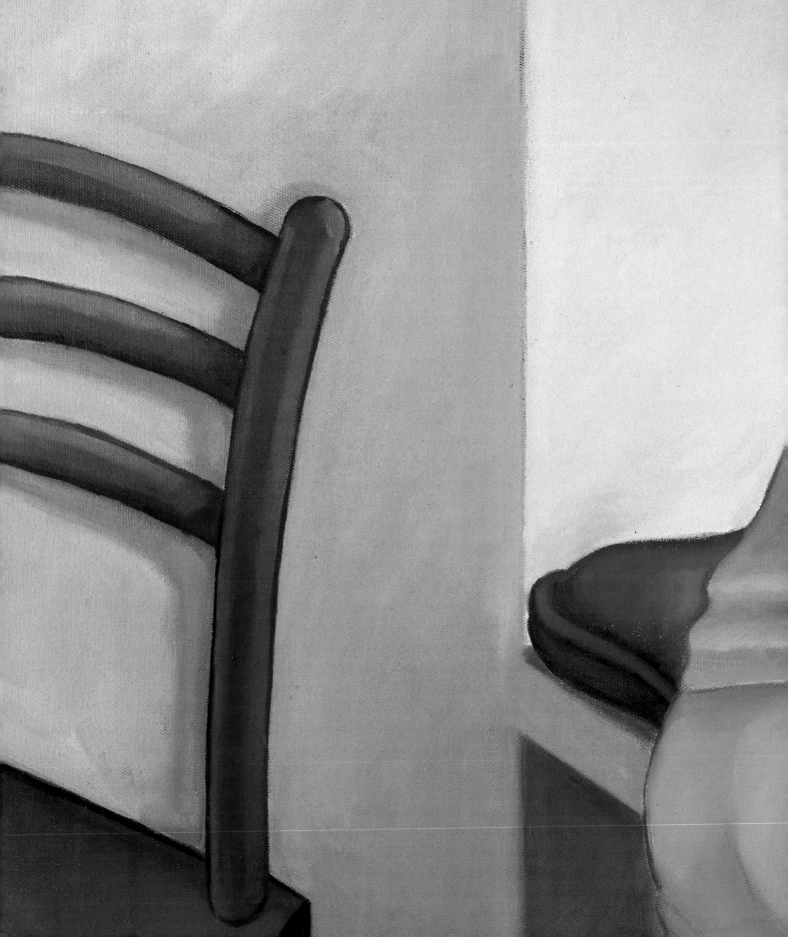

Looking down on the street

snow

Looking down on the street

trees

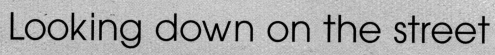
Looking down on the street

tracks

Looking down on the street

people

Looking down on the street

trucks

Looking down on the street

a friend

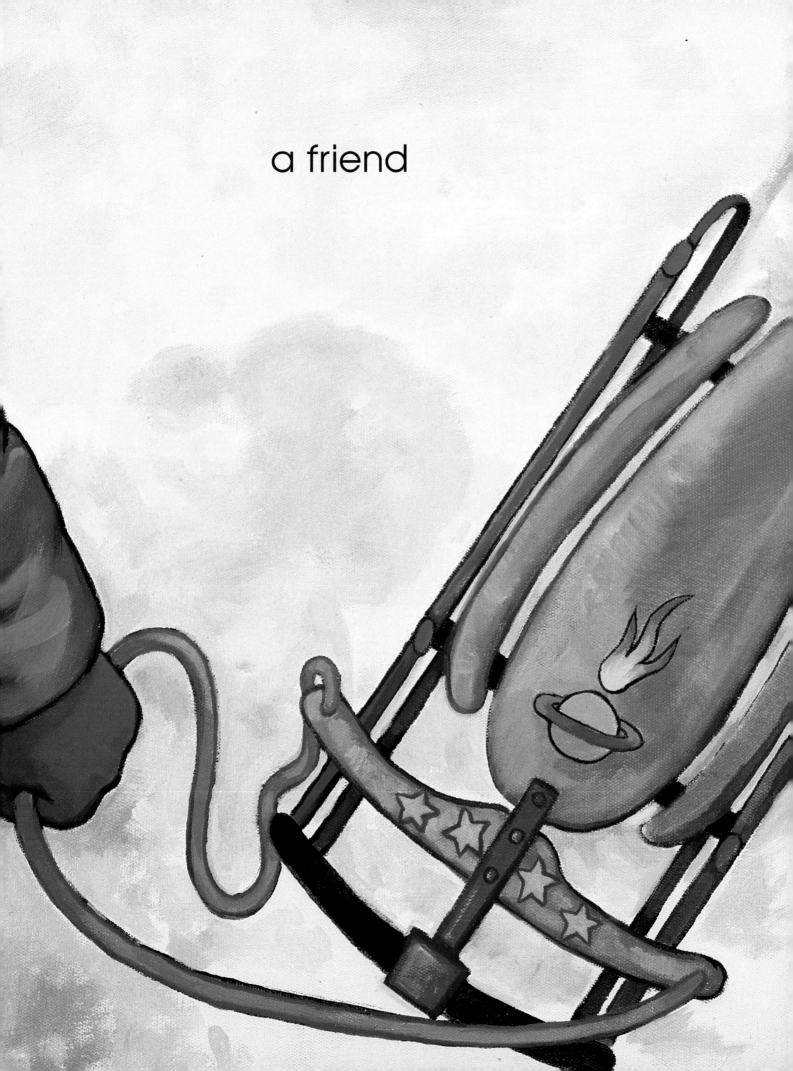

Looking down on the street

made me want to run down,
down,
down,

and out of the building to play.

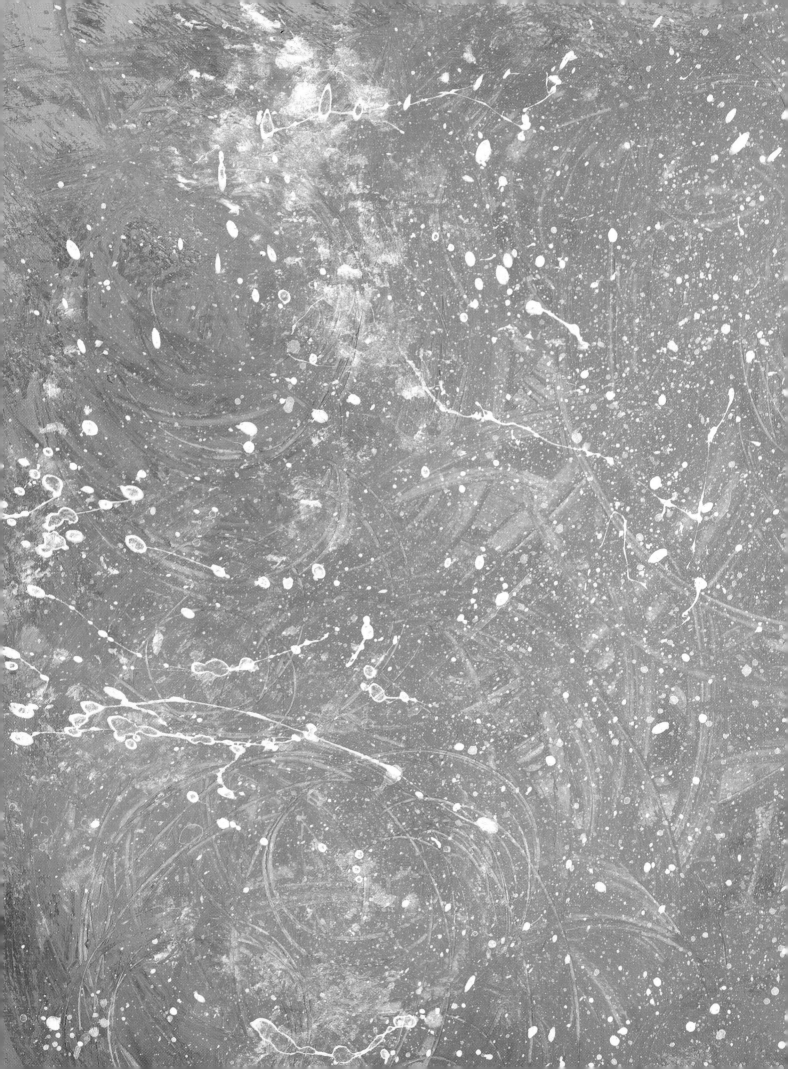

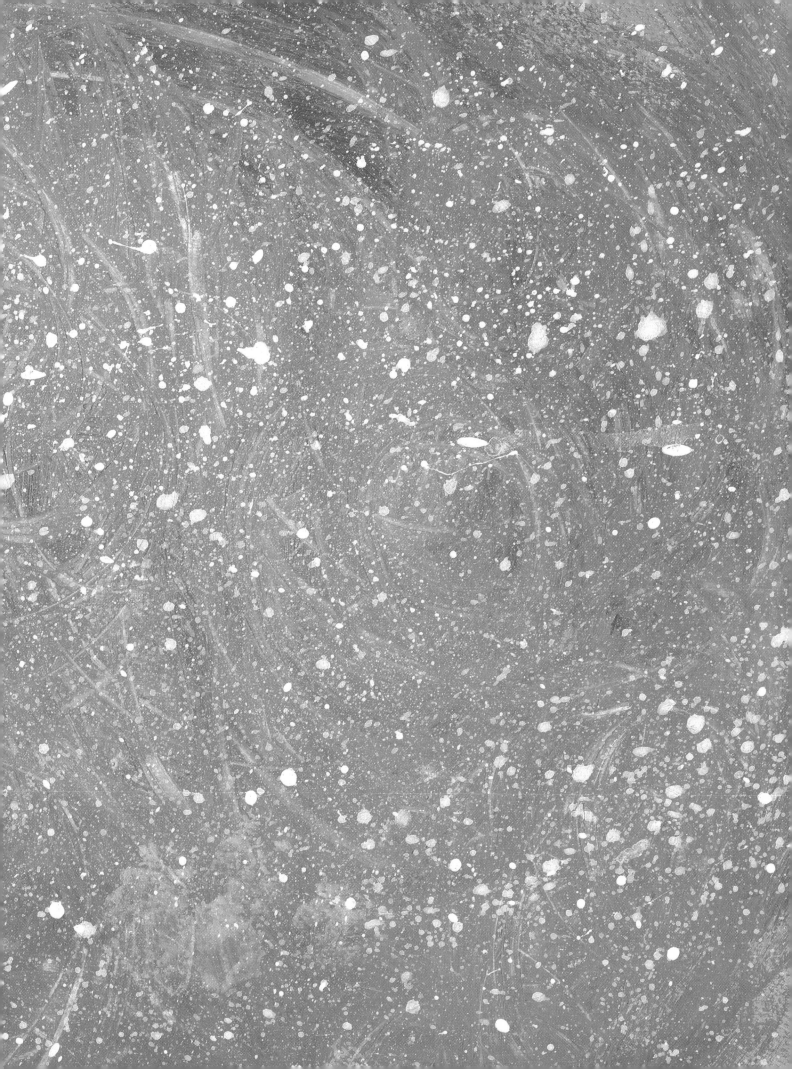